INTRODUCTION

It's ironic sometimes how life's daily events can inspire a dream. That's exactly what happened here. It began one cold night in High River, Alberta, when Ivan 'The Wizard' was visiting his son Jake 'The Hero' and his family. It starts with a neighbor calling the RCMP to report a 'suspicious smell of marijuana' in the vicinity; and ends with Ivan realizing his son had something to teach him about the medical benefits of cannabis; and ultimately the health care benefits for the masses. What happened in the middle is hilarious, inspiring, and now also employs close to 100 people across Canada.

We've learned that it's about getting healthy, not high; and removing stigmatism is just as important as furthering cannabis education.

We hope that you enjoy our story; and thank you for your purchase! This publication wouldn't be possible without the support of our clients.

Jake and his wife live in High River, down a long and winding lane,
with Kush the cow, and Gramma Mary Jane.
Gramma was getting stiff and old;
she couldn't really handle the cow or work in the cold.

Times were hard in High River - the price of oil was low
- there was no income; so, Kush the Cow would have to go.
Gramma told Jake,

"Take the cow to town and clean her up nice,

then sell her at market to get that good price!"

So, to market Jake went with Kush the Cow, to get Gramma some medicine and heal her somehow. As Jake made his way, Ivan the Wizard appeared by their side, petting and measuring Kush's smooth hide. **"Don't go chemical for medicine"** he said with a grin, **"For relief and great feeling - this is a win!"**

Jake admired the seeds, then traded the cow, there weren't any doubts lingering now. Ivan the Wizard tapped his wand on the well; and said a few words to complete his spell.
"Plant these seeds where they have room to grow, and marvelous stalks they shall bestow."

Back home with his seeds Jake ran as fast as he could, happy to know he could do Gramma some good. But Gramma was vexed when she saw Jake's seeds:

"This isn't the medicine Gramma needs! I sent you to market to sell a fat cow, and a Wizard I am to believe now?"

And with a swipe of her hand the seeds flew out the window!
Where under the moonlight the magic started to grow.
The seeds inched through the soil, and as the sun crossed the
sky, those magic seeds sprung up to the clouds up high!

In the morning Gramma gasped at the sight she did see;
there were three sturdy plants believe it be!
Two were female and one a stud,
both those girls were producing seed and bud!
Carefully Gramma took a bud, setting it in the hot sun to dry.
With all this magic it didn't take long to have some butter to try!
Smiling Gramma says:
"We'll need more for baking sweet Jake,
make sure to go up those stalks and save our stake!"

Jake looked way up that green stalk, through the thick clouds there was no way to see the top. Strong and sure he started to climb, over leaf and sticky buds that were plentiful and fine. At long last he climbed over the top; where he spied a castle of glass refracting light, and a dread-locked Giant, seemingly loving the plants.... Just then, Jake heard a loud voice say:

"Ganja...Green...Sweet...Love...
I see da beauty of the sweet reefer bud
Be it Medic, Be it Chronic...
I mash it up, makin all my sweet tonics"

Jake thought for a moment, he knew he had to wait.
He wanted all those seeds; Grammas health was at stake!
He crept past the nursery to where the Giant's seeds were stored;
he almost had what he needed, just a few seconds more!!
Just as Jake was about to pocket the treasure,
the Giant boomed out with great big measure:

Jake was aghast, he thought Bob would be mad,
and then he blew smoke in Jake's face and well, he was glad.
**"Embrace dat smoke mon, we be goin' on,
I'm a gonna show you tha power of dat sweet gange mon!"**

When that cloud did part, Jake was astonished!
All of Bob's workers were making tonics and
good products and not just for chronics.

"Some live with PTSD and even shell shock; and take it from me
- it's nothing to knock. Tell them to use this spray for their panic
attack, after a short time, their feelin's will be harder to crack."

"We're big on safe production here, be steady, be sure.
So, the medicine's how Mother Nature intended - clean and pure!"

"An alternative medicine for cancer?? Phoenix Tears all the way!
A creation from Rick Simpson, see it at phoenixtears.ca.
Whether it helps for appetite or keeps the pain at bay,
sometimes it makes mutated cells obey!"

"Your neighbor has tummy problems my friend, CBD is his new best friend.
With just the right dose, it could get him on the mend! There are many ways to
help your friends in High River, make sure you take notes, and always be a giver!"

"I'm Bob da Giant, mon, and I've given you da info; it's time you return to High River below. Always remember dis took time to discover, and consumption is all about irie education ma brotha! Be sure to keep minors at safe distance; and call out my name if you ever need assistance!"

"The oil in the bud will aid what ails, Jake my new friend, you must handle the sales. High River has hard times from the price of crude oil, with this package here, you'll have cash to unfoil!"

Back down the weed stalk Jake did descend,
to put Gramma's and High River's troubles to an end.
He sold his seeds and shared the knowledge he gained,
the people felt better and soon CBD was famed!

In no time at all, new business had begun, and shortly thereafter the investors had sprung. Hector the Investor knocked on Jake's door:

"Canada's largest cash crop you say?!
Do tell me more! It outsells wheat and durum as well!?
For the community and economy this is ever so swell!"

CBD and THC were the talk of High River, so much so,
it got the attention of law givers! They wanted so bad the
black market to erode, legalization opened so many more tax roads!

What we need to know it's not revenue or taxes, it's the health care benefits for all of the masses. With the help of Hector, the industry did thrive, better application, education, the whole country came alive! People embraced the power of CBD; and were no longer criminals for consuming THC.

We can all learn a thing from the lessons in this tale, and friends, there isn't one about an 'inhale'. Not every Giant is a killer it's true, and not every Wizard will try to fool you! As for Jake, his family and Gramma Mary Jane, they're baking up goodies down that long and winding lane. Even Kush the Cow was happy - the economy would protect her, thanks to Hector investing in that lucrative weed sector!

THE CHARACTERS

Ivan the Wizard – Ivan Lloyd

It's not often that someone starts a business from an RCMP visit to the house and turns it into a million-dollar business. That's why he's the Wizard. The Wizard has magic and sees opportunity in doing good for people.

Jake – Jake Lloyd

The catalyst for Native Seed Co., Jake and the Weedstalk, and for the gift of marijuana education to Ivan, Eva, and the whole team. Jake, you're straight up inspirational!

Gramma Mary Jane – Eva Melas

True to life, 'Gramma Mary Jane', Eva Melas came into the business equation having no cannabis experience. Eva has had the opportunity to hear thousands of CBD success stories, and through her experience, passion was born. That passion is now driving the business.

Bob the Giant

The Legend who inspires legends.

Hector

In Memory of and Inspired by Hector 'The Investor'.

JAKE AND THE WEEDSTALK

Text and Illustrations Copyright 2019 by Ivan Lloyd

Written by Ivan Lloyd

Co-Written and Edited by Sarah Munro

Illustrations by Christina De Liso

Story Conceptualized by Jake Lloyd

Published by Native Seed Co.

www.jakeandtheweedstalk.com

www.cbdbrandproducts.com

Printed in Canada

First Print April 2019

ISBN 978–1–9990320–0-5